Dolphy Dreams

RP Collado

Copyright © 2021 by RP Collado

All rights reserved. No part of this publication may be reproduced, distributed, or transmitted in any form or by any means, including photocopying, recording, or other electronic or mechanical methods, without the prior written permission of the publisher, except in the case brief quotations embodied in critical reviews and other noncommercial uses permitted by copyright law.

ISBN: 978-1-954341-79-1 (Paperback)

The views expressed in this book are solely those of the author and do not necessarily reflect the views of the publisher, and the publisher hereby disclaims any responsibility for them.

Writers' Branding
1800-608-6550
www.writersbranding.com
orders@writersbranding.com

CONTENTS

Trump 1
Out of Curiosity 2
Paradox of a Kiss 3
Agree to Disagree 4
Darkness that's Night 5
Nubis 7
efflorescence 8
UTD 9
Eyes wide open 10
Up to you and me 11
Smile when you say good-bye 12
Promissory note; 13
Indomitable resolute 14
In God We Trust 15
swept away 16
Cathedrals 17
Measure of a man 18
What are we waiting for 19
Truth, by George... 21
Feed the hunger, not the greed 22
Mirror image 23
Aberration 24
Just, in an unjust World 25
Hunting conservatives with a crossbow 26
for Glory's Sake 27

… That is the condition we are now in and that is why it is the duty of the Individual to rise to a higher conception of their capabilities and undertake again the function which only the Individual can perform, that of producing new spiritual-ethical ideas. If this does not come about in a multitude of cases nothing can save us.

Albert Schweitzer
(The Light within Us)

if you want to get to know someone, don't ask what they believe…ask them what they know, I know three things;

1. creativity symptom of wellness
2. where there is inspiration, there is hope and
3. 'the best of what Humanity has to offer begins and ends with a simple act of expression'*

from 'Writings on the Wall'

Trump

A celebrity of note,
not worth
no praise have
I to heap
just a pissant politician
and a guttercrawl, when
in the twilight hour he creeps -

into the world of men
he may ascend
surrounded by his sheep
but when he dies,
he dies alone
and may his bones be
buried Deep!

Out of Curiosity

Question in your mind is lit
sheds light on facile, feeble wit
like winds blow soft cross' baron plane
against the lot but not the grain

will be gone, misspent youth
hid behind a wall of truth
like a shadow puppet play
killing time till judgement day

from fatal flaw to final gasp
heart felt pangs too weak to grasp
and when time comes to take a stand;
to wheeled the force at your command

will you simply bow
to the powers that be . . .
out of curiosity?

Paradox of a Kiss

what sweet dilemma this!
such is the paradox
of a kiss
that blinds you
till you cannot see -
except for the way things ought to be

that fills you
to your depth and core -
yet always leaves you wanting more
that volatile mixture
of fever and bliss -
such is the paradox
of a kiss

Agree to Disagree

just when I feel I could brave
the ordinariness most people crave
I find myself most ill at ease
when the poet in me disagrees

He longs for that rarefied aire
and the lifestyle only few would dare
though i may beg to differ if you please
when the poet in me disagrees

but, alas when you share space
with some so bold
you simply shrug and do what you're told
so I defer most humbly to the whimsical breeze
of the poet in me,
should we disagree -

Darkness that's Night

some are born to wander
like gypsies they roam,
searching for something
that reminds them of home

with lines that are spoken
and pin-points of view,
I follow the traces
that lead me to you . . .

but only through the shadow of light
can we see
the darkness that's night -

winsome castles
starry eyed dreams,
a view of a lifetime
that's never been seen

time is a winner when you can't walk away,
the comfort of knowing
when there's nothing to say . . .

the future is hidden,
the past will not die,
all is forgiven,
don't even know why

there's pastures of plenty
for those with the means,
the rest share a field
of old broken dreams

to capture a moment without a fight,
a fast flowing rhythm
with no end in sight . . .

but only through the shadow of light
can we see
the darkness that's night -

there's a darkness that covers, a darkness that calls,
a darkness that lingers and a darkness that falls

but only through the shadow of light
can we see
the darkness that's night -

Nubis

raise your head up high my friend
for what appears to be
is not the end

open up your eyes and ears
and utter your psalm
so I can hear

yes, gather your wits and feel your tongue
and see your journey's just begun

prey, hear the sound
of your own voice
and soon you'll have reason
to rejoice

though many dangers
still await
I will guide you
to your fate

till you are safe for ever more
upon the sands of kingdoms shore!

efflorescence

one can either stand
still beneath the wheel
without a sign or mark

or learn to dance in the wind
while dodging
arrows in the dark -

UTD

it is . . .
the proposition of life
inverted;
to sit an stare at a wall
for years and years
and instead of learning
to accepting it . . .

and by accepting it, you then surpass

you give in and become the wall -

Eyes wide open

I couldn't read, I could only bleed
from every orifice, my fluids ran
until I discovered 'the joy of speed'
that's when my race began . . .

from Plato and Socrates to
Pythagoras and Euripides,
my boundaries grew,
they knew no bounds!

what I didn't learn from history
I gained from modern sounds . . .

like 'kinda Blue and a Love Supreme'
music that lifts the soul,
but I never turned my back
on that 'sweet old rock and roll'

words and music stimulate
both my heart and mind

if you can keep your eyes wide open
who knows
what you might find -

Up to you and me

open up your eyes,
to the prize
that's waiting just for you

better get wise now,
and open up those eyes

open up your eyes
and get wise to the lies
they're telling you

better get wise,
and open up those eyes . . .

and if the way things are
ain't the way things ought to be,
well then, can't you see
it's up to you and me!

and open up your mind,
see what you can find,
take time to explore,
open up the door . . .

and you just may find
what you're looking for -

Smile when you say good-bye

lost the bet, but no regret
as I wipe a tear from my eye
caught in the rain
and miss a train,
just smile
when you say good-bye

if she could stay
just one more day
we could give
it another try
but it's getting late
and this is not our fate,
so smile
when you say good-bye

hard to believe,
but it's time to leave
yes, I guess it's better this way,
the dice is tossed
and with fingers crossed,
let the chips, let em' fall where
they may . . .

and you can bet, I won't forget
Lord! you'd think it was the Fourth of July
so just be glad
for the time we had
and smile
when you say good-bye -

Promissory note;

not to be taken in by another phony grin
and to learn from my mistakes
and I will gauge my own success
by the efforts that I make

and when it comes to matters of the heart,
I'll refuse to compromise . . .
like the poor fool who falls victim to
a politicians lies!

Indomitable resolute

wars will seethe with constant rage
with bitter tears and
bloody stains
by my duty I am bound
and choose my moments
to engage

my strategy, a simple one
no hero's blood runs
through my veins
but unafraid, I stand my ground
and with a rebels yell,
I hit and run . . .

the choice to fight or face defeat
steadfast, I will seize
the reins,
as I strive forward to
the sound of
my enemies retreat -

In God We Trust

How shall I dispose of thee,
all at once or piece by piece?
should I cut short
its suffering
with quicken hand
and set it free?

or with time delay
and a measured squeeze,
to extend and
prolong its agony?

'to rule with mercy
or iron rod . . .
the joy it must be,
to be a God!'

swept away

a passion flower cannot assuage
the turmoil that has come of age

no amount of violets
can ease a heart
torn with regrets

what joy can a 'morning glory' bring
to a fractured heart
or a broken wing?

what solace can one hope to give
to a soul that has lost
its will to live?

Cathedrals

starting with a plot of ground
and a mound of virgin soil,
he picks a spot and
with his two
hands he begins
to toil . . .

sworn to build a monument
unlike any seen before,
that will stand the test of time
with stained glass frames,
and more . . .

What's beyond the reach of man,
where does his limits lie?

before he journeys to the stars
you'll find him reaching for the sky -

Measure of a man

not by office, title
or by the fortunes he may reap,

but by the souls that he inspires
and by the promises he keeps -

What are we waiting for . . .

you'd think it'd take more than just reason
to shine the light our way
under this veil of darkness
beneath this cloudy sky of gray
where there is no easy answers
only questions by the score . . .

years go by like a raging river
seasons seem to come and go
time melts down like a candle burning
and the next thing that you know
you find yourself in the thick of battle
on your back, flat on the floor . . .

neon lights up ancient cities
so we can see where kings once stood
we praise with honor, pride and passion
but it won't do us any good
they only set are thoughts to driftin'
back to the days of yore . . .

figures turn to one another
hanging tough and standing proud
as shadows fade into the evening
like the faces in the crowd
in honor of our fallen hero
lost to us on foreign shore . . .

so better gather your defenses
there's one more lesson left to learn
when all is done but for the cryin'
there won't be nothing left to burn
then you won't have to bother
to lock and chain your door,
still I can't help but wonder . . .

Truth, by George...

one cannot
refute,

greedy seed
brings forth
rottenest fruit -

Feed the hunger, not the greed

the hunger for . . .
a life worth living,
a nature for transcending,
and the spirit
for giving,

feed that ravenous,
carnivorous need
till there's not one more
hungry mouth
to feed,

gorge yourself to your
hearts delight,
and satisfy that
righteous appetite,

till you can't take
another bite -

Mirror image

your heroic figure you wave
at a whim
void of verve and of vigor
and no sign of vim

and when the dust settles
and the lights start
to dim

I see before me
the likeness
of 'him'

Aberration

breathe new life into the World
raise her from her temporal fen . . .

ease her fears with gentle sighs
till she's herself again -

Just, in an unjust World

note; to the
revolutionary guard;
orders given to proceed . . .

strike a blow to the
ruling class
target heart
and make
them bleed . . .

guide the family
down to where the royal wine
is stored

and as they voice their
solemn vows
give the Czar
his just reward -

Hunting conservatives with a crossbow

aim for their
egos and you
cannot miss

and seal
their fate
with a big
wet kiss

and let's
teach them
a lesson in
humility

by putting
them out
of their
misery –

for ted nugent

for Glory's Sake . . .

uncork those old
aspirations
and near vintage
dreams

reclaim the fire and
the sword
that once justified
the means

cast your gaze beyond
the peak horizon
to the far off
distant shore . . .

and when in line
for Glory's sake
know there's always
room for more -

He's an artist that has been around a while but has always operated under the radar. As an amateur musician and songwriter for over forty years he was most active in the 90's then suddenly, silence… for seventeen years, not a word… until now, that is… with the help of LDA and others he's been able to recover his voice and then some, and he seems to have a message to share with all… according to reliable sources, apparently; 'it's nice to be back'

RP Collado

www.ingramcontent.com/pod-product-compliance
Ingram Content Group UK Ltd.
Pitfield, Milton Keynes, MK11 3LW, UK
UKHW041957230426
12048UKWH00008B/384